I0576375

One 'n Done #2

Girls, They'll Never Take Us Alive

By
Matt Lydon

Published by

Read Furiously

Read Often. Read Well.

Published by Read Furiously. First Edition.

ISBN: 978-1-7337360-3-9
Quick Reads
Fiction
Satire
Heist
Crime Fiction

For more information on the One 'n Done series, *Girls, They'll Never Take Us Alive*, or Read Furiously, please visit readfuriously.com.

For inquiries, please contact samantha@readfuriously.com.

Edited by Samantha Atzeni

Read (v): The act of interpreting and understanding the written word.

Furiously (adv): To engage in an activity with passion and excitement.

Read Often. Read Well. Read Furiously

It was only a few minutes beyond 10am on Friday morning, and Joanie had finally had enough. The waitress hadn't been back to check on Joanie and her friends after dropping their omelets on the table with a hurried thud. Joanie fixed her mouth into a firm grimace, adjusted her prescription sunglasses and said:

"I'm gonna give this bitch a piece of my mind."

Her friends gasped, and while they had heard Joanie swear loudly and often at their weekly meetups, they were never quite prepared for that amount of sass from their octogenarian friend.

Diane, especially, was always taken aback. "Joanie, you can't. Just leave her alone. I didn't want that much coffee anyway."

"It's the principle of the thing, Di. You can't let these goddamn chippies get away with bad service."

"But--"

"No buts, I'm giving this owner a piece of my mind." Joanie slid slowly to the end of the booth's seat, and started to heave herself out into the aisle of the diner. Her bones, the seat, the table, all creaked with the motion of Joanie wrestling her way to an upright position. After about a minute of struggle, Joanie was on her feet, pocketbook slung over her shoulder, and stepping carefully up to the front desk of the diner, so as not to aggravate the corns inside her therapeutic sneakers.

"Joanie. Joanie, come back." Diane implored while Bette, their stalwart third breakfast companion, silently sipped on now ice-cold, weak tea from a chipped china cup.

Joanie only waved a dismissive hand as she shuffled toward the mints and toothpick dispenser on the cashier's desk. Diane began to fret and stage whisper loudly to Bette, who only raised an eyebrow above her cold teacup to Diane's quickening speech. The trio had come there for several years, since they'd met as ushers at the local theater. As all three were retired, they filled their days with activities and groups and outings, of which Friday Morning Breakfast Club was one of their favorites. They'd been coming to this particular diner, the Golden Sunrise Family Restaurant, for years, and generally liked the food and service. Over the last several months that level of service had entered what Joanie often referred to as a death spiral, or "circling the terlit drain." High turnover of servers, the recent death of the original executive chef and the changing of suppliers to a cheaper, down-market purveyor of lower-cost but still edible foodstuffs created a perfect storm that was about to crash open and flood downtown Croydon, courtesy of Joanie.

"Yes honey! Hello, my dear! How was it, your breakfast again this Friday morning, yes?" The morning manager, a paunchy, mustachioed Turkish man gliding toward 40, greeted Joanie with gusto, as he did every Friday. He smiled broadly at Joanie, but her grimace soon dimmed the wattage from his joyfully lit face. "Something wrong, my honey? Is Kristine not to your usual standard today? Please, tell Mutlu was is the matter." A few seconds of freighted silence passed between the venerable old gal and the younger man.

Joanie broke it open. "You know I've been coming here for years. Me and my girlfriends, every Friday. Get the same thing: thin blueberry pancakes for me, the feta and tomato omelet for Di, and the peppers and egg sandwich and carafe of tea for Bette."

"Yes, yes, my honey! I know! I sometimes write the order myself! What is--"

"Hold your horses, mac. This girl is the pits.

Messes up my order every damn time in the last 6 months, gives me a rash and shit when I ask for extra butter for my cakes, and can't be bothered to check on us more than once. I'm an old lady!"

At this, Joanie made a flourish with her hand, indicating all five feet and two inches of her slowly shrinking frame. The manager, Mutlu, was in rapt attention, but keeping silent to find where he could re-enter the conversation without being rude. More silence followed.

"Well? What are you going to do about it?"

All men make mistakes, and most make those mistakes on a small scale, more or less everyday. In the years that followed, observers on the scene would recall that the mistake that followed, "Mutlu's Mistake" as it was later known, seemed so obvious to avoid. Not having been raised in this country and around older white women from a certain class in that country, Mutlu's attempt at humor to diffuse the situation was ill-advised at best, and as it turned out in the worst case scenario, disastrously foreboding of what followed.

"My honey, I cannot make you less old lady. I can only hurry Kristine up more from her break. Kristine!" he broke off laughing, turning to the kitchen to call after the errant waitress.

Diane and Bette looked up from their table, eyes wide. As the doughy manager called for the waitress a second time, the morning mummering got more excited until someone uttered a scream. All noise stopped, except for the flat-screen TVs above the wraparound counter. The show was at the cashier's desk, though, and Mutlu would turn to find out.

He turned back to Joanie, only to find the small 80-something had pulled a silver handgun from her purse and was now brandishing it in his direction. "Alright, you. I want satisfaction! I want more hot coffee at my table NOW. I also want the round of rye toast my friend Bette ordered, brought with as much haste as this dumb thump of yours can muster. And another thing--"

Joanie turned toward the kitchen, mid-rant, but then... stopped. A look of confusion bloomed on her face. Joanie had lost her train of thought, and wasn't sure at which station she might have to disembark. "Damn it all! What was I saying?"

Mutlu, nanoseconds from the blunder of his life, reached out to calm Joanie down.

Joanie wasn't expecting any touch or human contact as she was lost mid-thought. Later, when she thought about it, she figured it must have been the trick nerve in her left elbow that hadn't healed right from when she'd broken her arm falling down the stairs at her son's house. But when Mutlu reached out and grabbed her arm, Joanie saw and felt the gun explode in her hand. A bright flash, an almighty racket and immediate deafness followed. Joanie shook her head, and suddenly, Di and Bette were in front of her, eyes wide with fear, mouthing something frantically that she couldn't hear. They started pulling her toward the door.

"-od damn it, Joanie! You can't just SHOOT a man!"

"Oh, I think Di's right there, Joanie. I mean, it looks like it was an accident, but those sneaky lawyers make it look however they want it to look. And not to mention--"

Joanie's head swam, doing an overhand crawl through the soupy haze she found herself in. Drowsy. Fuzzy, Loud. Unclear. Then:

"You still with us, Joanie?"

It was Bette, slapping Joanie in the face. Not hard enough to hurt, just hard enough to garner attention. Both women were in the spacious backseat of Diane's black sedan, while Diane herself was already behind the wheel, her white, arthritic knuckles on the steering wheel. Her voice quavered and cracked. "Where my going, Bette?"

Bette began to open her mouth but was cut off.

"Di, go ahead and go to the bank on Street Road. I have to make a withdrawal."

-- $ --

11:01 am, and the closed circuit TV above the waiting area in the neighborhood bank showed three ladies of a certain age trying to come in through the mantrap door at once. The teller manager behind the customer service desk saw the ladies, raised a hand in a gesture of halt, but then decided to just buzz the door open so all three ladies could come through at once. Regulations strictly forbade it, but these ladies had been coming in for years. Or so the teller manager thought.

The trio made their way to the teller lines, and as the bank was short-handed today, the teller manager returned behind the line to help out with the ladies' transactions. "Hey ladies!

How you? How YOU doin today? What can we do for you?"

The ladies didn't speak, and the teller manager's smile faltered. The one with the large, dark prescription sunglasses looked up a bit into the teller manager's face then grunted. Laughing, the teller manager said, "Well, you'll have to be a bit more specific than that." Leaning forward to the ladies, he chanced to look down, and realized what was in the sweet elderly lady's hand.

"Oh," he said.

"Everything you got behind the counter there, and never mind with the dye-pak, junior."

"Right away, ma'am."

-- $ --

Six thousand, eight hundred eleven dollars and 22 minutes later, Joanie and the girls were on the road. Di was driving her black sedan and swerving just a little, while Joanie looked out the window. Bette was in the back, divvying up the cash. "Girls, this is roughly twenty-three hundred each! We could make a day of it! What say Atlantic City?"

"Oh, no, I think we need to give ourselves

up, right now!" said Diane, perhaps a little too loudly from the driver's seat.

"You worry too much, Di," said Joanie. "Have a little fun once in a while. When's the last time you had fun?"

Di breathed heavily before answering Joanie. "I have fun every week with you girls. Our Friday dates, our nights as ushers at the theater, our--"

"Oh shit on all that!" Joanie cut her off. "I'm talkin' real fun. Boozin', gamblin', cutting a rug! When did you do THAT last?"

Joanie harrumphed triumphantly into silence as both Di and Bette were silent for a bit. Maybe it had been a while for all three ladies. Di thought it was unfair of Joanie to raise the issue of dancing. Di's husband had been gone for years, victim of an unfortunate incident with his stupid 1989 Corvette he was always pouring money into and Joanie knew that. But, why dancing? Joanie had both hips replaced in the last two years, and couldn't do more than shuffle between the couch and the dining room.

Bette, for her part, played a spelling game on her smartphone with her granddaughter, who was off skipping class at Penn State. The silence in the car became palpable. Diane finally said, "I know! C'mon girls, ROADTRIP!" Diane swung the car around in a wide U-turn, scaring several motorists in downtown Croydon.

"Where we goin now, Di? Did we decide?" asked Joanie from the backseat.

"The boards in Ocean City, ladies. I feel like some sun, sand, and coffee!" Diane practically sang.

"Eureka! 10 points!" Apparently, Bette was all in for this idea.

-- $ --

Marla shifted in her tollbooth seat and reached for the sponge in the dish that kept her fingers moistened to handle the money drivers paid as they went their way deeper into the body proper of New Jersey. She was seven hours into an eight hour shift and was already mentally checked out of the workweek into her weekend. She and her girlfriends were headed to Ventnor for the weekend, just to relax on the porch, maybe go to the beach. Whatever the girls' plans were, there was going to be as much white zin as each of them could handle all weekend long. One more hour to go. Come on, baby.

A black Honda Accord with an EAGLES vanity plate on the front with the word MIMI emblazoned under the disembodied eagle head slowed into Marla's lane. Looked like two old gals, but Marla laughed and caught herself. She was 53 and with two adults sons herself. She wasn't exactly young. She was smiling and *tsk-tsking* herself when the Honda rolled up to her window.

"Five dollars for your two-axle car, ma'am," Marla said with a smile still playing on her lips as she opened the cash drawer. She turned to the lady in the driver's seat, and stopped smiling. The old bird in her BluBlocker sunglasses was pointing a gun at her.

"Listen, *MA'AM*," the old lady began, "I'm not trying to rob you, I just want you to let me and my friends through here for free." She ended her sentence with a nervous nod and pursed her lips, as if that would be enough for Marla to comply. It might have been, if Marla followed Port Authority protocol like she'd been taught. Somehow, Marla knew today wasn't a day for protocol.

"Where yas going, ladies?" Marla asked, now seeing both a lady in the passenger seat

11

and another lady in the back. All three were somewhere north of 70 if Marla had to guess. From the back, the lady who seemed the oldest said, "Ocean City, honey. Why, you trying to come with?"

The driver with the gun turned around, and hissed, "Joanie! What are you DOING?"

"Relax, Di. Either she's gonna report us or she's gonna come with."

"But--"

"You worry too much. How about it, toots?"

Marla had had guns in her face over the years and she'd often just wave those drivers on through, as Port Authority cautioned them to do. *No use losing your life over something as small as a toll*, they said. *Cost of doing business loss*, they said. *Just always follow protocol*, they said, and *everything would be fine*, they said. Marla was okay with that and could have done just that, but again, today wasn't a day for protocol.

"Sure. Is the back open?" asked Marla as she flicked the switch that turned the green arrow above her booth to a red *X*. She looked down on the cash drawer, grabbed all the paper bills that added up to something like 3300 dollars and left the booth, stepping around a barrier and into the open back door of the black Honda. She hated this job, but if she told it just the right way to the police later, she could probably massage some pity for a scared, older lady from the dull investigators at Port Authority or the State Police.

Besides, Marla's friends were all kinda boring. Three old ladies with a gun seemed like a much better option, even if they were going to dry old Ocean City.

"Let's roll, ladies," said Marla. "It'll be a few minutes before the troopers get back from lunch, so we'll have about a 20 minute head start. Just press that gas pedal down... Di, is it?"

The three friends clapped and as Marla sat down in the back next to the gruff one who seemed to be the leader. Marla looked at her. "Alright, Di. You heard her. Floor it!"

Diane floored it through the toll plaza and towards the New Jersey shore points.

-- $ --

June of 1967. Joanie Hall and her best friend Bette Camarotta lean against the railing on the boardwalk in Sea Isle City, NJ. Joanie is wearing a sleeveless light green plain top, with white pedal pushers and her long blonde hair tied up off her face with a red bandanna. Bette, in a solid navy blue shirt with grey plaid pedal pushers of her own, lit a cigarette and offered it to Joanie.

"Get that out of my face, Bette. It's unladylike. Don't you want to attract a man?"

Bette shrugged, took her own drag, and said, "I've never had much trouble, Joanie. Besides, Eddie's my backup at home. We're here for our OWN little vacation, aren't we?"

Scowling, Joanie snatched the smoldering stick from Bette's mouth and sucked angrily at the butt while giving Bette a severe case of the sidelong glance.

It was true. Joanie was bored in the city and needed something novel. The school year was over, and she'd just finished year two of teaching fourth grade at St. Edward's in North Philly. A powerful ennui had settled in at her summer job at B. Dalton's bookstore, and she had suggested to Bette that they take a few days off and see what there was to see down the shore. Bette agreed, as her own shifts at the King George II Inn were easily shed. Moreover, Bette suggested they crash at her grandmother's place in the Pine Barrens on the way to Surf City. So now, here they were on the boards in Sea Isle, lounging, smoking and so far, lacking any real contact with any fresh young fellows.

Bette looked over at Joanie, realized she wasn't getting her original cigarette back, and lit a fresh one for herself. "Joanie, what if we just took a drive up and down the main drag a bit? Maybe stop somewhere for lunch? I'm getting up a bit of a hunger and this cig ain't helping much. What you say?"

"I guess I could eat. But--"

Just then, a yellow kite smashed right into Joanie's face, temporarily blinding her and tangling in her hair and bandanna with a papery *thwack*. Joanie yelled and yanked the offending kite off her face, taking the bandanna and a couple of stands of her hair with it. Bette's eyes were wide, her cigarette hanging precariously off her lips. A laugh played around her eyes, and crept around her mouth, but Joanie caught her.

"No, Bette. Nevermind about this. WHOSE KITE IS THIS?" Joanie yelled.

Seconds later, a kid ran up with a spool of thread in his hand. This redheaded kid was dressed in a striped t-shirt with some zinc-oxide on his nose, sandals struggling to stay on his tubby feet. This child was about to feel her wrath, but something was familiar about this kid.

"Oh gee, sorry Miss Hall! I didn't see you there!" Dennis Gallagher, rising fifth grader, had been the bane of Joanie's teaching existence from early September until two weeks ago when school let out. The constant questions, the furtive chewing and sticking of gum under the desk, the near-constant bothering of the girls in various ways, not to mention the general slovenliness of young Dennis, were constant challenges to Joanie Hall. She hadn't turned to drink yet, but more and more, Joanie decided this might be the vice to help soothe her soul after a long day of Dennis.

"Oh, hello… Dennis," Joanie said, trying to inject enough of her schoolteacher warmth to hide the roiling fury surging up through her chest. "Family vacation down here in Sea Isle, huh?"

"You bet, Miss Hall! Mom says it's going to be the last vacation I take for a while. On account of school and all."

"Why is that, Dennis?" Dennis was an idiot,

and Joanie knew it, but had tried to boost his grades just enough that the nun in charge of the teachers at Saint Ed's would okay passing him on to the next grade. Dread filled Joanie, even before Dennis confirmed it: "Sister Helen wrote on my report card that I gotta repeat the fourth grade. I guess I'm kinda stupid, huh?"

Bette smiled from ear to ear behind her cigarette and sunglasses as Joanie looked from Dennis to her friend and back. Despite her dislike of Dennis and the approaching torture of having him for another year in her classroom, Joanie softened at the child's mention of his own stupidity. While it might be true, it always broke her heart to hear a kid say it. Even if the kid was a moron. Honest tears of compassion welled up in Joanie's eyes.

"It's okay, though, Miss Hall. I'm gonna have help, though!"

Joanie's eyes widened, and she can't stop the question: "What do you mean, Dennis?"

"See, that's the great thing, Miss Hall! I'm gonna have you to help me AND my little brother Chucky is going to be in the fourth grade, too!"

In the ensuing 40 years of her teaching career, Joanie Hall was never written up for unprofessional behavior, nor would any parent of any child that came through her classroom ever blame her for being anything less than impeccable in her speech, actions and mannerisms. The thought of having both Dennis Gallagher and his younger brother Charles, a boy given to setting things on fire and indiscriminately reciting lewd limericks he learned from their father in the same classroom at the same time was too powerful a catalyst for the rage and sorrow that braided themselves together and roared up out of Joanie in that instant.

"FUCK!" Joanie screamed, and even though it shouldn't have been possible with the crowded boardwalk and the roaring Atlantic behind her, that epithet echoed, and for a split second, everyone stopped in their tracks and looked in her direction. Fathers looked disapprovingly on, while mothers covered their younger children's ears, and mouthed "how dare you" at Joanie. Dennis, for the first and last time that Joanie would ever see it, registered a look of silent shock on his face. Then, he bent over and picked up his mangled kite.

"Uh, sorry, Miss Hall. See you in September, I guess," he said before hurrying off to join his unseen family.

Joanie stared dumbly after him. Would he tell his parents? Would they call the school? Would she still have a job when she returned to the city? Her rage transmuted to fear and worry.

"Great, yelling 'fuck' in front of a kid. Nice going, Lenny Bruce. How about we take that drive now. Maybe look into getting some sneaky pete?"

"Deal. Lead the way," said Joanie. The girls hopped into Bette's Plymouth Fury, and turned onto Landis Ave and headed north, out of Sea Isle.

-- $ --

MILES AWAY in Ocean City, Di Humbert was trying to enjoy a short vacation with her mother Alma, before she retreated back to her legal secretary job in Philadelphia. "Mom, I'm going to get a popsicle, do you want anything?"

"I'd like a Mai Tai, Di. Get one and bring it back here."

"Mom, Ocean City is dry, you can't get a Mai Tai in town, let alone the beach. How about a popsicle?"

Diane's mother, Alma, turned toward her daughter, sighed, and said, a bit more forcefully, "Diane, I'd like a Mai Tai. I don't care what you need to do to get it, just get it for your mother."

Not wanting to anger her mother further, but rolling her eyes as she went, Diane walked up to the boardwalk in hopes to complete her mother's request. She knew that there was no liquor store here, nor anywhere within Ocean City limits. She'd known it since that time when she was 14 and her father had asked her mother the same thing, but for a fifth of scotch. When Alma had come back empty handed, Diane's father had already left the shore house, telling his daughter something about *getting tight* in Avalon. She didn't know what that meant. Di would come to know that "getting tight" seemed to also involve disappearing on your family for long stretches at a time. She thought about getting tight on her mother right now. Avalon wasn't that far away and this was already a crummy vacation. But there was a little coffee shop, so she went in.

"Hello, there. Can I get you something, hun?"

A teenage girl with high cheekbones, straight dark brown hair, and a ridiculous pink and brown waitress uniform with matching pillbox hat smiled so hard in Di's direction, it made Di uncomfortable. "Uh, well, my mom wants a Mai Tai, but I can't get that here, can I?" Di asked.

Impossibly, the coffee waitress' smile got bigger, and she said, "Oh, well! We can't do a Mai Tai, but we do have an excellent bourbon maple coffee flavor that the owner has just come up with! If you close your eyes and breathe deeply, you can almost imagine drinking a hot toddy in a cabin with your future husband!"

Di laughed quickly and freely, but immediately regretted it when she saw the earnest waitress' face crumple. She sputtered to follow up and undo the damage. "Oh, no, I'm sorry, I didn't mean to--I mean, that actually sounds kinda nice. Does he have a beard?"

The pink and brown clad young woman asked coldly, "I'm sorry ma'am, who? Our owner?"

"No, no. My... future husband."

The smile returned to the coffee waitress' face, and she leaned forward over the counter again with the same level of joy she'd had when Di entered the little coffee shop. "If you want him to, then yes! What do you say, you want to give it a try?"

Di nodded, and then asked, "What's your name? You seem like a fun person."

"Oh, it doesn't matter, does it? It's a little weird, but it's a family name, so I'm kind of stuck with it," she said as she poured Diane a mahogany-colored, aromatically intense cup of coffee. Di took the cup, sipped a little to see if it needed some sugar or half-and-half. It didn't; it was delicious. She closed her eyes and smiled ear to ear. Then she opened her eyes and said, "So? What's your name, dear? Mine's Diane."

The waitress frowned a little, though her eyes kept smiling. "It's Traute, but I tell people it's Trudy. Like on my name plate!" Traute/Trudy thrust her chest forward, with her gleaming nametag.

"Ah, das is gut!" said Di.

Trudy replied, "Oh, do you have German family too?"

"Well, Pennsylvania Dutch, but close enough. My own father's name is Emil, and I have an Uncle Klaus."

"Oh! My father's name is Klaus and my husband's name--" At this point, Trudy broke off, and Di raised an eyebrow. Was this girl old enough to be married?

"Sorry, my ex-husband. He left after I got pregnant with our daughter."

"Oh, I'm sorry, I didn't mean to pry."

"No, it's fine. It's a while back now. She's seven."

"Your husband is--"

"No, silly. My daughter! Her name is Marla."

Trudy brightened up again, and told stories about how sassy and smart her daughter Marla was, but that she worried she would be a bit wild, growing up without a father. Di protested and put her hand on Trudy's and looked into her face. "Well, she seems to have a wonderful mother, so I don't think she'll go wrong."

The two women looked at each other for a few sweet, silent seconds. Gulls called from the beach, while families and singles walked by on the boards a few feet away. Trudy was the first to pull away.

"More coffee, dear? I can refresh your cup for you, free of charge!"

"I could use a refresh, but hey, how do you get the flavor?"

"Company secret, Diane. But come back

23

tomorrow morning, and maybe you can ask the owner himself!"

"I think I can do that. Mother and I are here until Friday."

"Come in about 7. Dad gets up early for the breakfast rush, then surf fishes on the back bay the rest of the day."

"The owner is your father? What should I call him?"

Trudy suddenly became grave, and said in a voice that was much smaller than it had been this entire time. "Mr. Schleifer. He doesn't like to be called anything but that. He even makes me call him that in front of customers. I still call him 'Papa' at home."

Diane immediately felt closer to Trudy. Sometimes, other people also have fathers that leave a lot to be desired. And mothers, for that matter. "Hey Trudy, can I get one more cup, perhaps to go, for my mother?"

"12oz or 16oz, dear?"

When Diane got back to the beach, with a larger coffee than she'd ever seen in her life, her mother was gone from their spot on the beach. The blanket was still there, and the umbrella was still open, but Alma was nowhere to be seen. Diane turned her head to look up and down the beach, but could only see kids running up and down the sand, sunburnt fathers laying underneath newspapers, and mothers in coverups listening to transistor radios. Teenagers were braving the sea and threatening to splash each other with the cold Atlantic water. Though her mother was missing, Diane looked around, and smiled. She put her lips to the coffee she'd bought her mother and began to sip.

"What the hell are you doing, Diane? And is that my Mai Tai, or no?"

Diane sighed to herself, turned around to her mother, and said, "It's coffee, mother. No alcohol in Ocean City, but if you close your eyes and take a deep breath, you can imagine it's like having a brandy on the porch back in Willow Grove."

Alma scowled, took the coffee, and gulped right away. As she hacked up the very hot coffee, Diane turned away again, laughing to herself. *Take that, Mother*, she thought.

-- $ --

"Hold on, Di. I need to stop in here," Marla said from the backseat. Diane brought

25

the black Honda to a rolling stop in Circle Liquors, overlooking the bay and the traffic circle headed into the dry town of Ocean City beyond. Bette turned and asked if Marla wouldn't mind getting her a fifth of gin and maybe a plastic "squeezy" of lime juice if they had it. "Sure, doll. Anybody else?" Di declined, and Joanie grunted in what might have been a *no thanks*. Marla smiled and slid out of the backseat toward the store.

"I don't think I trust her," said Joanie, adjusting her sunglasses.

"Why not, Joan? Now who has to relax?" asked Diane.

"Who trusts a woman who can just pocket a till like that and walk away from her job? I tell ya!" Joanie responded.

Diane, for her part, had been a bank teller manager for most of her professional life, and if she could find it in her heart to forgive the funny woman who'd joined their crew an hour ago, then maybe Joanie should be able to. "Besides, Joan, who should trust an old hag who shot a nice young man over cold, thick pancakes?"

"Old hag, huh?" Joan's eyes immediately narrowed, as did Diane's, behind each woman's massive BluBlocker sunglasses. Not that anyone inside or outside of the car could tell. A silence settled over the car, tense and humid, barely ameliorated by the bay breeze blowing in through the downed windows of the Honda.

Diane felt like speaking, but then backed off. Joan started, but retracted into her backseat. Then leaned forward again. Diane, white-knuckled on her steering wheel, clenched her teeth in anger, boiled to say something. Joan, silently and invisibly frothing in the back, felt similar. Each woman's tension bubbling up, fast, now faster. The silence mixed with the hot air choked both of them until--

SNNNNnaararrrgghghhg.

"Jesus Christ!"

"Hannnhh. What?" Bette said as she stirred from a nap she'd lapsed into while her friends were fighting.

"Oh Bette, your narcolepsy!" worried Joan. Diane also clucked sympathetically over the drowsy Bette, and in so doing, the two women forgot their quarrel over the fourth.

"Oh, where is Marla?" Bette asked, still clearing the narcoleptic nap fog out of her brain.

"In the liquor store there. Why, did you

need something else?"

"No, just wondering."

"You did ask her for a fifth of gin before she got out of the car."

"Did I, now? Huh. I mean, I guess I could use a Tom Collins, or even a gin rickey."

"There was the lime, too. You asked her for lime."

"Right. You did, Bette."

"Well, my seizure brain must have known what I wanted before I conked out. Let's drink to that!"

"Yes, let's! Speaking of, where's that Marla gone to?"

All three women looked toward Circle Liquors, hopefully to catch sight of their traveling companion, who'd been gone at least 10 minutes, which sometimes felt like an eternity to these ladies, and other times felt like too short a time to get anything done. That was old age, for you, though. One thinks they'll be quick when they reach their seventies or eighties, but the reality is they're just as slow as the people they made fun of when they were young. It's why they sent Marla in; she was positively youthful at 57 and had a spring in her step when she'd hopped into the back of Di's car many miles ago. But maybe, after the initial excitement at the tollbooth, Marla, too, was worn out and needed a rest. *Take your time*, each lady in the car thought. *We're not going anywhere.*

-- $ --

The three friends assessment of Marla was generous, and too kind, it turned out. At the same time Joanie, Bette and Di were waxing fond of Marla from their position in the parking lot, Marla herself was inside Circle Liquors and telling the clerk to call the police. In only 30 minutes in the car with the three old gals, Marla had heard enough complaining to last her the rest of her lifetime. Joan's sciatic nerve problems sparred, sort of, with Bette's narcolepsy and high arches. Diane complained of a bad back that had sidelined her for years, but which hadn't actually hurt her since she'd lost a bunch of weight about 15 years ago. She had grown tired of complaining about her ex-husband so she moved to the back thing, which was new information to Bette and Joan. Joan asked if it was as painful for Diane as her own bunions had been, which set off an

8 minute discourse on the wonder of proper orthotics and how those could change one's life. None of this information was something Marla had ever cared to know, although she did take a mental note about orthotics for her shoes for when she got back in the tollbooth. Sometimes, that standing got to be murder.

Eventually, though, the conversation took that turn in that way that old friends have of looping around in the conversation to where it began, with Joan's sciatic nerve. This proved to be the spot where the ladies landed on Marla's own last nerve, and she decided to drop that dime on these sweet, annoying older ladies.

As Chad phoned Ocean City Police Department, Marla looked out the window at the black Honda. It was late afternoon, getting on toward fall and the close of the beach season. The soft jazz Chad played on the store stereo complemented the sun as it had slowly begun its descent into the back bays, swathing Ocean City and the rest of the barrier islands in a richly-hued golden hour. Marla took out her smartphone and began taking pictures of the car with the old gals inside it. The light glinted off the patchy black paint job that featured on some of the cars from that model year 2002. She zoomed in, took pictures of all three girls laughing. She zoomed out, and took a picture with a filter on it that made it look like a scratched Polaroid. She took another snap with filters that put rainbows and clouds on it, but didn't like that and began scrolling to find something she liked. She found one, with a dog's ears and tongue wagging, and was about to take a picture, but something was wrong. Marla began yelling.

Chad looked over at Marla from his continuing phone conversation. "Could you hold on, please?" said Chad to the police on the other end of the phone. "Ma'am, what's wrong? You can't yell in here, this is a liquor store!" Chad ventured, cautiously.

"Yeah, sorry about that, Chad, but the reason I came in here? The reason you're on the phone? They're GONE!"

"The three ladies who ran the toll at--"

"Yes, Chad, the ones who robbed me at Burlington. They're fucking GONE! Tell them that!"

Chad turned his attention back to his phone conversation, but then handed the store phone's receiver to Marla. "They want to speak to you, I think," said Chad as he handed off the phone.

Marla took the receiver, and stared stonily at Chad. "Hello?"

"Ma'am, are you the victim of the robbery at the Burlington-Bristol toll plaza?"

"I am, listen--"

"And is your name Marla Jenkins?"

"Yes it is, but I--"

"And do you reside at 321--"

"HOLD ON!"

"Ma'am, I'm trying to get all the facts, and your interruptions are only slowing me down."

"Yes, sorry, Officer, but--"

"No buts, ma'am. Just confirm a few more things for me, and I'll gather the rest of the information I need to conduct our investigation. Now…"

The phone call lasted another seven minutes, while Marla recounted many details of her life for the investigating officer. Details, she believed, that were totally irrelevant to the matter at hand. So when Officer Jutland finally arrived at the crux of the matter, it took Marla by surprise.

"Let me repeat myself, Miss Jenkins: Where are the ladies now?"

"I don't know."

"But the clerk told me you had them in line of sight."

"Yes sir. That was 11 minutes ago, before he handed the phone to me, and you went off on your fishing trip."

"So you don't actually know where they are right now?"

"No. I was watching them get in gear and drive off, when you asked me to come to the phone."

"Why didn't you say anything, ma'am?"

"I did, but you kept shushing me and saying my interruptions were slowing you down. So, I watched Di's car pull to the edge of the parking lot, but didn't see which way her blinkers were indicating she was going."

"..."

"I'm sorry, sir, I didn't catch that. Cat got your tongue? Regretting your shushing me now, aren't you junior?"

"Ma'am..."

"Don't ma'am me, sir. I'm old enough to be your mother from the sounds of it."

"Ma'am. I mean, Miss Jenkins--do you have any idea of where they might have gone?"

Marla smiled for two reasons. First, she'd silenced a man when he was trying to exert his

33

alpha male dominance over her. She'd lived too long and with a succession of too many dumb men who thought they were right to give away the opportunity to make such a dummy shut his pie-hole. Second, she was about to get in another dig.

"Oh yes, I do. And it'll be right up your alley, officer. Bring a mug."

-- $ --

Bette wore a slinky black dress, all the way down to the floor. Her hair was piled high, and pulled into a tight, intimidating beehive, with two lengths of her dark hair framing her face in an echo of Jackie Onassis. It was close to midnight, but Bette wore sunglasses that made everything on the verandah of the King George II Inn that much darker. She lounged against the railing, took out a cigarette and began to smoke it. Herb was out of town, and she was playing the cool, leonine housewife, out on the prowl for younger men. Playing only, because Bette didn't want the hassle of actually having to go through the motions of courtship, sex, lying, sneaking around. She didn't want to do that to Herb, certainly, but more importantly, she was just bored sick of the dumb drama it caused. All her girlfriends were either getting divorced or else living in sham marriages because they'd had a few kids and didn't want to break the little darlings' hearts. Her own kids were fine, if a little on the stupid side most days, but she felt if she and Herb split, Herb would be just fine taking care of the kids by himself. They were old enough that they fed and dressed themselves, and Herb was never a guy to foist off his daily routine on someone else like some of these helpless saps out here. It's part of what attracted her to Herb. He was a fully formed man, and she, a fully formed woman. Neither had time for nonsense. They did have time for fun, and kids, as it turned out. Just part of the adventure.

But Herb was in Pittsburgh for work, and on leaving he said to her, "Bet, have a little fun this weekend. When the kids go down to sleep, sneak out. Get up to something! Just, don't do anything I wouldn't do."

Bette smiled, and kissed him, and said, "You got it, bud."

Bette was still lounging, and took a long, slow drag of the cigarette, when a guy, maybe in his 20s, maybe a little bit older, came up

35

and came onto her. "Say I couldn't help but notice you're here at this mixer alone. What's a pretty lady like yourself doing alone in a place like this?" said the young man, his sandy hair swooping ever so slightly into his eyes.

Bette grimaced at the awful come-on, then laughed. "You gotta try harder than that, junior. Rachel doesn't respond to such pedestrian parlay."

Rachel was the character Bette had come up with for when Herb was out of town. She was mysterious, always dressed in black, with those matching sunglasses. She never went out before 8 in the evening and she never compromised on whatever it was that she wanted to do. She took no guff, gave no quarter, and left a string of broken young men in her wake. Oh, and she also referred to herself in the third person.

"You have one more chance to impress Rachel, plebe, before I take leave of you." Bette took a measured, slow drag from her Pall Mall. "What's the last book you read?"

This question caught the young man off-guard. He stammered, and his young brow knitted in confusion and consternation. Bette looked at him behind her sunglasses, smiling. When the seconds of feverish rubber facial expressions from the young guy spiraled out into a minute, Bette's left eyebrow rose above her sunglasses. She hadn't expected to cause him this much stress, but she was enjoying this. After a few more moments of watching his brain flop around behind his agonized face, she leaned in, and said, "Are you not a reader then, Sunny Jim?"

The young man's face went slack, then almost immediately brightened up again. "Wow, how did you know my name was Sonny? Are you a mind-reader?" The smile returned to his face, and Bette turned to unseat the cigarette from her lip and feign a cough. She was really hiding a laugh behind her hand, and as she coughed once or twice more to provide a more believable cover, she thought, *Boy, this kid is good and dumb. Shame to waste the night by dismissing him now.* Then she came up with an idea.

"Tell you what, Sunny Jim," Bette began, "I know this little late night bookstore where we can look at books together. If we time it right, we can sneak some coffee and read in the stacks until they close at 2. Or," and she paused for effect here, as she saw him swaying hypnotically to her words, "whatever we can think of to do in the stacks other than reading,

if you have ideas."

That hint of a suggestion was enough to animate Sunny Jim, or Sonny, or whatever the lunkheaded youth's name really was, into loose-limbed action. He swept Bette up in his arms, which Bette noticed were sufficiently muscular, and nearly carried her across the verandah to the steps down to the street. "My car's just over here, Miss Rachel!" He tugged on her hand like a boy-child about to show a friend something cool.

Bette, however, had played this game more than once. "Hold on, there, buddy boy," she said, crossing her arms. "How do I know you're not a serial killer like the Zodiac Killer? Preying on defenseless ladies at dance mixers and then leaving weird clues for the police to find?"

This question seemed to shock him more than the question about reading. "Uh, uhm… uh…"

"For all Rachel knows, you've been watching Rachel for weeks, following Rachel to and from work, making notes of her movements and drawing pictures of Rachel for your bedroom wall."

"No, Rachel, I mean, Miss Rachel, I'm not a--"

"Creep? Who's to say? Didn't seem like you knew anybody at that mixer."

"But I did! My friend Joey is the--"

"What? Doorman? Valet? Line cook in the kitchen?"

"... yeah. He's the doorman. But he got me in for free and--"

"Oh, so you're cheap, huh? Can't pay your way into a mixer to find a nice girl to treat to a night of drinks and dancing?"

"I thought you wanted to go to a bookstore and make out?"

"This is 1971, a lady's allowed to change her mind."

"Oh, right, sure, I didn't mean--"

"Uh huh. I *bet* you didn't mean!"

This last bit struck both of them as a bit nonsensical, and Bette and Sunny/Sonny stared at each other, Bette daring him to move, and Sunny/Sonny praying to god the beautiful woman made the first move so he'd have any idea at all of what to do next. She did make that move.

She swept over to him, his mouth grew huge and happy in response, and he opened his arms to receive her, but she expertly put her index finger on his top lip, buttoning it with a

shhhh. "Let's go for a ride in your car. Rachel needs to feel the wind in her hair."

Seconds later, they were in Sonny's car, a 1951 Studebaker Starlight coupe. There was no ragtop, and the car shuddered into gear so slowly, you might have been forgiven for thinking a few people were actually pushing the car forward. So, the wind Bette actually felt in her hair was a result of her own breath ricocheting back on her from the too-close windows in the Studebaker. Sonny barely got the car up the short incline from the parking lot to the street, but when he did, and finally got some downhill to help, the car's engine finally did groan into a semblance of life.

"We're riding now, Rachel!" he beamed from the driver's seat.

Bette, for her part, rolled her eyes behind her sunglasses. It was so dark now that she barely saw anything on curbside as they passed through the old, narrow streets of Bristol.

"I know a little spot at the end of Radcliffe Street where we can go and watch the geese fly against the moon," Sonny offered.

"Take me there in your chariot, good citizen!" Bette said, choking back a little laugh.

As the Studebaker wheezed up Radcliffe

Street toward the abandoned shipyards, Bette played with the glove box in Sonny's car. "Oh, don't do that, please. There's trash and some other stuff in there that could spill out," said a nervous Sonny.

"Oh I'll be gentle, and I'll clean up anything that spills out," said Bette, as she fingered the knob on the glove box, a bit suggestively.

She reached out and tweaked the knob, and the glove box fell open. Some tissues, a ballpoint pen and a copy of the *Army Survival Field Guide* fell out, as well as a pearl-handled .22 caliber pistol that landed neatly on her lap. "Oh geez!"

Bette was nervous now, not mock nervous, but actual nervous at seeing the gun in her lap. Without knowing quite how or why, she scooped up the gun and pointed it at Sonny. "So, this has been your game all night, huh? You're some sort of rapist or ruffian that thinks he can take advantage, huh? Well, not TONIGHT, bucko. Not on Rachel's watch! Pull the damn car over!"

Sonny reached for the gun, but missed, and grabbed a handful of Bette's right breast. Shocked, Bette squeezed the trigger and shot him. The bullet passed cleanly through Sonny's hand and lodged in the driver's side panel, just above the crank for the window.

"Ah damn it, you shot me! Why the hell did you shoot me?" he whined as blood started leaking out both sides of the newly-minted hole in his hand.

Bette knew it was an accident, but she was already playing a role, so she improvised the truth. "Look, Rachel doesn't take crap from anyone, especially when they grab for a pound of flesh. You pull this car over right now, and get out. No more funny business or the second shot won't be a warning!"

Sonny did as he was told. Bette locked the passenger side door, then slid over to the driver's side, locking that as well.She rolled down the window slightly. "Listen you, Rachel's going to let you live, and it's only about a mile and a half back to the King George. You'll make it back there in 15 minutes, maybe 10 if you run."

"What about my car?"

"Oh, this? This and this little bugger, " Bette held up the .22, "are my souvenirs from tonight. If you play along now, you'll find your car in the morning, not far from here. The gun? You're not getting that back."

"But that's my dad's car. AND his gun!

He'll be so sore at me!"

"You play with the big dogs, prepare to be pissed on, junior," Bette said. She wasn't sure if this was the appropriate adage to use here, but her own father said it alot, and it seemed to fit the occasion. With a wave of her hand, Bette put the car in gear, and Sonny watched dumbly as it slid out of the shipyard lot, making a right turn up Radcliffe to follow the river path.

Twenty minutes later, Bette was walking away from a boat slip further up Radcliffe into the next town, as the Studebaker's rear-view lights vanished slowly into the darkened Delaware river. She tucked the little gun between her pounds of flesh, took off her heels, and crossed the street barefoot. The street was deserted at this time of night, even though it was Saturday, and walked toward the front door of the only house within 1500 feet of the boat slip. She dug down the front of her dress, past the gun, and produced a set of keys. These she put into the lock, turned, and walked into her own living room. She walked down the hall to check if Cecilia and Warren, her kids, were in bed. The phone began ringing. Curious to see who it was, Bette picked up the receiver, as she slid out of her dress and took off the tight beehive wig she'd been wearing all night long. "Hello?"

"Bet, my love! Figured you might be getting in right now. How's my girl?" It was Herb. Dear sweet Herb! "Get up to anything interesting tonight?"

"I did. Wanna hear?" Bette asked, as she twirled the pearl-handled .22 around her index finger.

"No, love of my life. I don't want to keep you on long enough to wake the kids. Remain mysterious. I'll be home Tuesday. Client apparently wants to show me the best steakhouse in Pittsburgh, then there's some all-company meeting on Monday morning they want me at. Can I bring you anything from Pittsburgh?"

"Just yourself, Herb. Hurry home. I love you."

"Will do, Bet. A thousand kisses, and good night!"

That Herb. He always knew how to treat a lady.

-- $ --

"What? Hurry home? We just got here,

44

Bette!"

Joanie was rousing Bette from her nap in the backseat. Bette sat upright in the front passenger seat of the Honda, and turned to find the driver's seat empty. Diane had already gotten out of the car. The smell of the back bays was in the air, and the *rat-a-tat* cry of gulls careened overhead, but it seemed to Bette that the car wasn't anywhere near the beach. Looking past Joan, all Bette could see was gravel, a dark brown wooden barrier fence, and the tell-tale tall weeds leading into a swath of saltmarsh just beyond the white of Joan's capri-pants.

"Where are we, Joan? I thought we were going to the coffee company?"

"In a bit. Di wanted to walk out onto this godforsaken mush for some reason here."

"Oh, does she like the smell of the bay?"

"This? It stinks. Don't know what she could see in it anyway."

"Eh, well, we'll see. At least there's no kids out this way. No kites to get caught up in."

"Geezus Christ. You ever gonna drop that? That was what, 20, 30 years ago?"

"It was longer ago than that, Joanie."

"The hell it was!"

"Oh it sure was. Back before I met Herb, back before you got married. You know, back when we didn't have to pick our funbags off the floor before getting into the shower."

Both Bette and Joanie laughed, and Joanie slapped her lightly on the shoulder. "Damn you to hell. Still funny after all these years."

"Truth in comedy, Joanie. Truth in comedy."

"Alright, then. Let's go find Di."

The two women walked slowly and uneasily across the salt marsh to find their friend. It was late September, and the season had already cooled, leaving the marsh a little more solid than it would have been at the height of summer. Still, the mud squirted and oozed around their white sneakers as they walked through the tall reeds calling out Diane's name. A breeze that had blown up made it hard for Bette and Joanie to hear, but then, faintly, they heard a response.

"Here, girls! I'm right out here!"

After stepping around some thick links of chain and a hefty portion of rope cast off from an old anchor, Joanie and Bette emerged on a sandy stretch of the salt marsh that was easier to stand on. Diane stood near the ocean, her face up toward the sun and her arms low at her sides, but somewhat outstretched, trying to catch the last rays of the afternoon September sun. Joan hobbled over first, while Bette looked backward into the salt marsh for something.

"Whatcha doin, Di? Why did you want to come here?"

Diane let her arms fall to her side, and she toward Joan. "I came here to see that," said Diane, pointing to the edge of the water where she sat on a rock. Joan approached, not understanding, and after looking at the rock, she still didn't understand.

"So, a rock on the inlet. Big deal," said Joan. "Can we go now?"

Diane looked hurt, then took Joan's hand. "Just another minute more, Joanie. Please. I need this."

Joan looked at Diane, and saw a tear rolling down her friend's face. "Alright, then. If you need it. I'll be over at the car," Joan responded.

"No, could you just… stay here with me one more minute?" asked Diane, squeezing her friend's hand.

Joanie nodded, and Diane turned back toward the rock and took up her sun-soaking position again. Joan pushed up her sunglasses to rub her eyes, and as they slid back down her nose, she looked at the rock Diane had shown her. Now, Joan saw some writing, and leaned closer. A heavy hand had inscribed "Chuck =n= Di, 1969" and Joan didn't understand. She knew Di had gotten married in 1969, but her ex-husband's name wasn't Chuck. Or was it? Joanie felt that fuzziness from earlier in the day return, and turned away, momentarily slipping Diane's grip. The fog rolled into Joan's mind, but a clammy scrabbling at her hand brought her back into the sunlight. She was flummoxed, and looked up to see Diane's face, wet with tears, crying silently in front of her.

"Di, what's going on. Who's Chuck and--"

Diane reached out a finger and put it on Joanie's lips, while pursing her own, and shaking her head. Di's eyes were red and glistening from the crying and Joanie knew her friend was in pain, but couldn't think of a reason why. She felt the need to ask who this Chuck fellow was again, rising in her throat, but she decided that seeing her best friend cry like that wasn't worth knowing the little truth that led to a secret hurt. Sometimes, our physiology forces us to forget for the sake of survival. Sometimes, we need to choose that forgetfulness for the sake of love.

Joanie, caught somewhere in between both, chose the latter, and hugged her friend. "It's ok, Di. I got you now."

As Di and Joan embraced, Bette walked over with something in her hand. "Girls, I think I found a friend!" Diane and Joan dropped their hug, turning toward Bette who was holding a box turtle in her hands. "I found her under a log. Or him, I guess. But I think it might be a her. She didn't bite me when I picked her up."

Joan, not sure she cared for having a turtle around, asked, "So, what are we going to do with him? Take him with us?"

Bette began to answer, but Diane cut her off. "Yes. Let's put this little bugger in my car. We need to make it over to the boardwalk soon anyway, before the coffee shop closes."

Joanie shook her head, but Bette thought it was a great idea, so back toward Diane's black Honda they went. "Well, if we're gonna have a mascot, shouldn't we name it? What do you say, Di?" asked Bette.

"Sure, we can do that! How about Boxy?"

"What about Leonardo?"

"Or maybe Tur-DELL? Hanh? Whaddaya think?"

Suddenly, the box turtle craned out its

neck, and bit Bette on the hand, causing her to drop the amphibian and accidentally kick it into the reeds of the salt marsh several feet from Di's car.

"Damn it all! Little bugger! We didn't even HAVE you that long. I would have let you go!"

Joanie turned to Diane with a twinkle in her eye, and said, "Well, seeing what just happened, I think it *is* a girl, and we better name her Marla."

"Yep," said Di. "Leave the bitch. She can find her own way back to the liquor store."

Despite the pain in her hand, Bette joined the chorus when all three of them laughed. The ladies piled into Di's car once more, put on their seat belts, and headed for the boards on 9th or 11th Streets. They could still make the 5 pm closure of the coffee shop if they hurried. Marla, both turtle and human forms, be damned.

-- $ --

Officer Ed Sheeran, no, not *that* Ed Sheeran, was perplexed. He'd gotten the call on the radio about three old women who'd robbed a toll plaza in Burlington and taken a hostage.

He'd never heard things line up just this way before and he was still doing the internal math on it. Sure, women were offenders less often than men, but not all that less often when you come right down to it. Every once in a while, a dummy got it into his head to rob a toll plaza, thinking the money would be easy to get then to haul ass out of there with the other cars for cover. Too much chaos, and when the idiots did try it, they almost always crashed into other cars. For the one time in a hundred that they didn't, the cameras on the toll plaza caught their make, model and license plate from so many angles, the perp couldn't help but admit it was his car they'd caught on film. Unless of course the perp had stolen the car, then… but that was a whole other crab trap of fun.

Bank robberies, check fraud, petty theft, grand theft auto. All of these were things he'd dealt with. But a hostage situation? Ed had never dealt with that before and there wasn't much call for a negotiator in Ocean City. The only hostages people tended to take here were cruiser bicycles from the boardwalk vendors. Even then, the would-be thieves realized that without a bike rack on their car to affix the ill-gotten bike to, their getaway was a no-go.

This was a real live, honest-to-God hostage, though. The woman working at the toll-booth was kidnapped by this group of ladies, or at least that's what the dispatcher had said. Photos from the toll-plaza seemed to indicate there was a gun involved, so these ladies were considered armed and dangerous, but then the detail followed that these women were all retirement age or older.

Why were grandmothers breaking bad, Sheeran wondered. It boggled his mind, but Sheeran wasn't much for imagination. He might daydream every once in a while, but it was mostly about laying in the hammock in his backyard, after he'd trimmed the lawn with a push mower he inherited from his dad. He liked order, and so these grandmas being out of order bothered him.

He radioed back to dispatch, "Copy that. Will look for 4 ladies in a black Honda accord with PA plates. Over?" Nothing came in for about half an hour while Sheeran made his rounds, stopping at Ocean City High School for a bit to talk to the retired Marine who served as a crossing guard there. Then Sheeran pointed his cruiser south along the main drag to see what might be going on in the South end of town. As he neared the bridge that led to Strathmere, Sea Isle City and other points south toward Cape May, the radio crackled back to life.

"OCPD HQ to all units, please be advised we have an update on previous APB regarding 4 women in a black Honda. Hostage has been released at Circle Liquors in Somers Point. Unclear if suspects headed north toward Atlantic City or south toward Cape May. Suspects still considered armed and dangerous. Proceed with caution. Repeat..."

Sheeran turned the volume down on the squad car radio. He'd heard it fine the first time. So, the old ladies were in the neighborhood, then. As lacking in imagination as Sheeran was, he could, however, extrapolate several scenarios from incomplete data. This was imagination unto itself, but Sheeran never looked at it that way. Instead, he saw this skill as something necessary in the course of his job. Let the creative stuff get sponged up by that Hamilton guy, or Bruce Springsteen, while he patrolled the badlands of the shore. He caught himself and laughed at the thought. He wasn't on Childwood's PD, writing ordinances for showing one's underwear to the boys who couldn't be bothered to pull their pants up on vacation.

No, he was on the case, thinking that the ladies could go across on the Garden State Parkway, into Beesley's Point and Marmora, which would be out of his jurisdiction. Atlantic 559, Shore Rd and Route 152 would all put it out of his jurisdiction too. The only way it would become his problem is if the Old Lady Perps, as he'd begun to think of them, came across Route 52 directly into the heart of the town. If they were at Circle Liquors, Sheeran felt reasonably sure that they'd be coming that way, and so turned his car around in the type of illegal U-turn that only cops get away with, and headed for Bay Ave to hopefully intercept the old ladies.

As he turned up 21st Street to head toward Bay Avenue, he saw the sign for Uncle Bill's Pancake House and realized he hadn't eaten today. Uncle Bill's was already closed at 4:30, but Sheeran wondered if he couldn't grab a quick sandwich at Wawa. Ocean City wasn't that big, and he figured he'd be able to catch up to 3 old ladies in a black Honda no problem. They hadn't gone to driving school like every cop in this town had, although he didn't like the idea of starting a high speed chase in town. Still, these were grandmothers, and you never knew. Maybe they wanted to go out in a blaze of glory, or floor it from the Bay Ave bridge through the guardrail near Corson's Inlet, and smash into the Atlantic Ocean, like a wet, East Coast Thelma and Louise.

But that was ridiculous. Leave that up to someone with a bit more imagination, Sheeran told himself, as he pulled into the Wawa on West Avenue. Six minutes later with a meatball sandwich in hand, Sheeran strolled out to his cruiser, only to hear the radio calling his name. "PO Sheeran, respond. Are you in the vicinity of boardwalk and 11th, over?" Sheeran fumbled his sandwich through the open window of his cruiser, and yanked open his door and sat down, grabbing for the microphone. "This is Sheeran, I'm en route, now. Over."

"Ladies from tollbooth plaza robbery in Burlington have been spotted on the boardwalk. Proceed with caution. All available units, rendezvous at boardwalk at 11th street. Repeat, proceed with caution. Ladies are armed and dangerous."

Sheeran's stomach made a hollow gurgle, reminding him again how he hadn't eaten, but

there was no time for that now. The perps -
the old ladies - were at the boardwalk. His
own grandmother used to get him a box of
Fralinger's Salt Water Taffy for his birthday
every year, so maybe they were headed there?
The season was basically over, so it wouldn't be
likely the store staff had much cash on hand
if they were going to rob the store, but maybe
they were just going to get some salt water
taffy. Sheeran's stomach gurgled again as he
switched on the dome lights on his cruiser. He
didn't turn on the siren, though, as he liked the
element of surprise. Also, he didn't want any
pedestrians to see what was about to happen
next.

In a flash of hanger, that hungry state of
anger, Sheeran bit through the wrapping into
his meatball sandwich, spraying marinara sauce
onto his cruiser's computer and down his
patrolman's shirt. A bit of melted provolone
leaked onto his badge, obscuring the number.
That first mouthful Sheeran chewed down
was almost equal parts printed wax paper and
sandwich, but the immediate relief to his barren
digestive organ improved his mood so much, it
was as if he'd sat down to a surf and turf dinner
in Atlantic City with the boys. With one hand

on the steering wheel, and the other gouging open the sandwich wrapper the rest of the way, Sheeran careened his cruiser through the late afternoon streets of Ocean City, gobbling as he went in search of grandmothers on the lam.

About one minute later, the sandwich was done, and Sheeran glanced down, noting the wreckage of the sub all over his shirt. A passerby could have been forgiven thinking Officer Sheeran had been shot, and needed to tend to his wounds. Another cop would shake his head and grin, knowing that if a CO had seen him, he'd immediately write him up for conduct unbecoming. You just didn't go around with stains on your patrol shirt. That was rookie stuff, not veteran cop stuff. Sheeran brushed the big crumbs off with his free hand, then grabbed the sandwich wrapper to scrape off the remaining globs of sauce and cheese. He was nearly at the boards and was really scraping the provolone out of his badge when he careened past an open spot and rear-ended someone's parked SUV. The airbag in the SUV inflated, but his own cruiser's bag didn't deploy. He thanked God for small favors, climbed out of his cruiser then looked for anybody eyeballing him on the street. Nobody. Good.

That would just slow him down. He had old ladies to catch up with. Sheeran started up the boards at a brisk walk, but heard sirens from another approaching unit. So much for the element of surprise.

Sheeran broke into a jog, and looked into the window at Fralinger's. A woman behind the counter, and two younger people pointing at different taffies in the case. No dice. Sheeran continued on, and jogged past Ocean City Coffee, and ducked in, the bell hung just above the door jingling as he entered. Jane, one of the year-round regulars was behind the counter. "Hi, Ed! Jamaican Me Crazy today?"

"No, Jane, sorry. I'm actually looking for three ladies who are part of an APB. Robbed a toll plaza in Burlington about an hour or so ago."

"Oh my god! That's terrible! Well. I haven't seen anybody rough like that, but there were three sweet old gals that just left with their new mugs. Probably still right outside on the boards if you wanna check. Something weird about them, though."

"What's that?"

"They had a bag of popcorn with them. Who drinks coffee and eats popcorn?"

"Couldn't say, Jane."

"Oh well, nice seein' ya, Ed!"

"Ok, thanks, Jane. Gotta go."

"Ed? You have time for a cup of--"

"No, Jane. Police business. Some other time."

"Suit yourself. Go catch the bad guys. Or girls."

Sheeran left the coffee shop, his stomach gurgling again as it fought to digest the paper and meatballs of his quick lunch without liquid assistance. The roasted beans smelled so good, and he would have liked to have a 16 oz of Jamaican Me Crazy. It was an exotic drink that made Sheeran think back to a vacation he'd taken with a girlfriend long ago. Twenty one years old, the girl, likewise, an all-inclusive resort, and 10 days to just soak up everything and anything on offer. Full open bar, swim up bar, cabana with table side bar service. Room service. Laundry service, if you got your vacation clothes dirty. Tanning beds, if you preferred doing your tanning outside of the Caribbean sun for whatever reason. Coffee that smelled like what Jane had held out to him in the shop came to the room every morning, and even though the girl was asleep and had worn them both out the night before, that aroma woke her up so fast it made Sheeran's head spin. "Eddie, drink some coffee, and then we can take a shower, and then head to the beach. Or maybe," she drawled this part out each morning for nine mornings, "we'll just stay here and figure out something to get into."

Imagination was one thing, but memory built from experience was another, and that girl's memory was strong even fifteen years later. Nobody called Sheeran "Eddie" anymore, and he couldn't even remember what the girl's name had been. Each time he smelled that coffee, though, it took him back. *Maybe I need a vacation after this*, thought Sheeran as he jogged down the boardwalk.

Sheeran was so deep into reverie about Jamaica, coffee and the girl whose name he didn't remember that he ran right past his quarry. Competing thoughts have a habit of distracting you, especially with such a powerful sense memory in mind. But then, hazelnut coffee, even with two extra shots of raspberry syrup isn't enough to rouse a man from daydreams of island nights with a warm, willing woman of wild ways.

The three of them, Joanie, Bette and Diane, sat on the boardwalk bench, looking out over the sandy stretch preceding the deep, dark Atlantic. As the light faded into the low buildings of the shore town behind them, each woman in turn dipped her hand into the bag of popcorn to grab another handful of the warm, salty pop, shot through with a touch of caramel and white chocolate. Each kernel was as checkered as they'd become in the last twenty-four hours. Diane took sips of her Ocean City Coffee, from a glazed red mug she had bought along with her coffee, while Bette took pictures with her phone and Joanie just stared off into the soft, deepening gloom of the salt sea.

Sirens sounding faintly in the distance drifted closer and the three looked at each other, a look of worry in their eyes even as smiles played around their lips. Each woman in turn looked into the eyes of the other two, trying to see what they were feeling without having the courage to summon up the will to just simply ask. Joanie's eyes, ever behind her prescription transition sunglasses, remained impenetrable but she broke the silence by leaning forward and saying, "Girls, they'll never take us alive."

All three ladies were still laughing three minutes later when four officers from two Ocean City PD squad cars from the Ocean City PD loaded them into a cruiser and drove them away. The arresting officers couldn't understand why these old gals decided to break bad now, at their ages. In spite of themselves and their position as officers of the law, the officers shrugged and laughed along with the ladies all the way to central booking.

A Note to Our Furious Readers

From all of us at Read Furiously, we hope you enjoyed the latest installment of our One 'n Done series - *Girls, They'll Never Take Us Alive*.

There are countless narratives in this world and we would like to share as many of them as possible with our Furious Readers.

It is with this in mind that we pledge to donate a portion of these book sales to causes that are special to Read Furiously and its creators. These causes are chosen with the intent to better the lives of others who are struggling to tell their own stories.

Reading is more than a passive activity – it is the opportunity to play an active role within our world. At Read Furiously, its editors and its creators wish to add an active voice to the world we all share because we believe any growth within the company is aimless if we can't also nurture positive change in our local and global communities. The causes we support are not politically driven, but are culturally and socially-based to encourage a sense of civic responsibility associated with the act of reading. Each cause has been researched thoroughly, discussed openly, and voted upon carefully by our team of Read Furiously editors.

To find out more about who, what, why, and where Read Furiously lends its support, please visit our website at readfuriously.com/charity

Happy reading and giving, Furious Readers!

Read Often, Read Well, Read Furiously!

Look for these other great titles in the One 'n Done series

What About Tuesday
by Adam Wilson

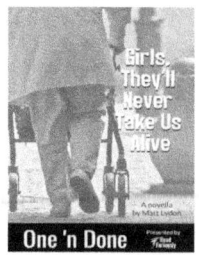

Girls, They'll Never Take Us Alive
by Matt Lydon

The Hero and Trauma
by Samantha Atzeni
Coming Spring 2020

Helium
by Adam Wilson and Jeff Chin
Coming Summer 2020

www.ingramcontent.com/pod-product-compliance
Lightning Source LLC
Chambersburg PA
CBHW071136100726

47908CB00008B/2612